Cat and Dog: A Tale of Opposites
This edition published in 2021 by Red Comet Press, LLC, Brooklyn, NY

First published as *Une histoire de contraires*
Original French text and illustrations © 2020 Tullio Corda
Published by arrangement with Balivernes éditions
Translation by Taylor Barrett Gaines
Translation © 2021 Red Comet Press
Art direction by Michael Yuen-Killick

Library of Congress Control Number: 2020948390
ISBN: 978-1-63655-002-2

20 21 22 23 24 25 TLF 10 9 8 7 6 5 4 3 2 1

Manufactured in China

RED COMET PRESS

RedCometPress.com

CAT & DOG

A Tale of
Opposites
Tullio Corda

Red Comet Press • Brooklyn

Awake

Asleep

Brave

Afraid

Slow

Fast

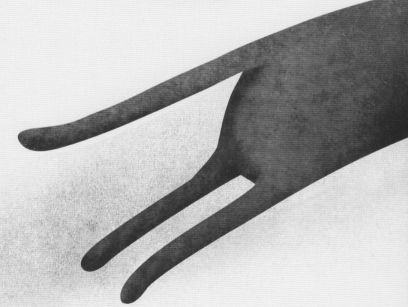

Below

Above

Upset

Unconcerned

Inside

Outside

Closed

Open

Near

Far

Up High

Down Low

Nimble

Heavy

Quiet

Loud

Oops!

Phew!

Soft

Happy

Sad

Enemies?

Friends!